CW00846966

This book belongs to:

_____

_____

Published by Poggle Press, an imprint of
Indigo Timmins Ltd • Pure Offices • Leamington Spa • Warwickshire CV34 6WE

ISBN: 978-0-9573501-8-2

Text © Luke Swann 2014
Illustration © Becka Moor 2014

All rights reserved.
Luke Swann and **Becka Moor**
have asserted their moral right to be identified as the author and artists respectively
of the work in accordance with the Copyright, Designs and Patents Act 1988.

10 9 8 7 6 5 4 3 2 1

This book is sold subject to the condition that it will not, by way of trade or otherwise, be lent, resold, hired out or
otherwise circulated without the publisher's prior consent in any form of binding or cover other than that in which it is
published and without any similar condition, including this condition, being imposed upon the subsequent purchaser.

www.springboardstories.co.uk

Rosa's Code

Luke Swann

Illustrated by
Becka Moor

A Poggle Press publication

For Susan Swann, who has been
both my mother and my father.

Rosa Franklin was not your typical girl. She was tiny and timid, with a shock of bushy red hair and a rather unusual interest in foxes. She spent a lot of time on her own and could usually be found with her head in a science book. Grown-ups often told her that she was unique.

Rosa knew that this was rather a silly thing to say, of course. Every girl and boy was unique. They were all made up of their own special code. So why was it that all the other children seemed to fit in? Rosa was fed up of standing out. She just wanted to be like everyone else.

Rosa didn't have any friends at school but she did have one special companion, a fox by the name of Dr Watson. His tail was as red and bushy as Rosa's hair but he never had a whisker out of place. He was quick witted, charming and wise – everything that Rosa wanted to be. They got along magnificently.

One Sunday afternoon, Rosa bumped into Dr Watson on her way back from the library. As they walked along, Rosa chatted excitedly about the discovery of a new supermassive black hole. Suddenly she was interrupted by two loud voices coming from a nearby building.

Dr Watson ran over to see what the commotion was, closely followed by Rosa. Spotting an open window, the pair peeped inside, their ears pricked.

'*Our breakthrough at last!*' a man exclaimed.

'*We did it. We're going to be rich!*' shouted a woman.

The building was a laboratory and there were two scientists inside. One of them, a spindly woman with grey-white hair as dry as a broom, did a little dance as she cried out:

'At last we've mastered the human genetic code. Now we can create perfect people!'

Rosa's eyes lit up as bright as the moon. *'Dr Watson, did you hear that? This might give me the chance to be just like everyone else!'* she whispered.

Rosa and Dr Watson waited anxiously until the scientists
had left the lab, then clambered through the open window.
There in front of them was the answer to Rosa's problems...

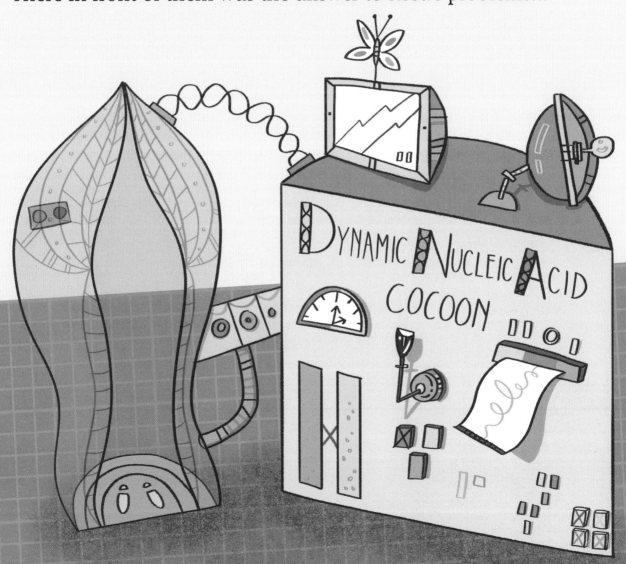

Rosa stepped into the magnificent machine. There were two big buttons inside – a blue one labelled EFFINGO and a red one labelled TRANSFIGURO. Rosa had no idea what the words meant. They hadn't done Latin at school.

Which button should she choose?

Red looked risky. Maybe it was best to play safe. As she pressed the blue button there was a loud buzzing sound and a sharp flash of blue light. Rosa began to sing to calm her nerves.

'*Remarkable Rosa I shall now be,*
Was once forgotten so easily.

Radiant Rosa with stunning looks,
Forget computer codes and books.

Regal Rosa how I will act,
Goodbye old Rosa – your bags are packed.'

She waited. And waited,

and waited, and waited.

DYNAMIC NUCLEIC ACID COCOON

But absolutely nothing happened. Rosa felt exactly the
same as she had all her life. What a terrible disappointment!

The next day as Rosa walked into the school playground something remarkable caught her eye. She gasped so loudly that a small bird nearly toppled from its tree. Standing right there by the climbing frame was a girl who looked just like her. Just like her, except somehow better.

'*Wow, Rosa, you've managed to control your hair at last!*' the prim and popular Pandora Peterson said to the new Rosa. '*You know, maybe we wouldn't mind you joining our Inner Circle after all...*'

'*Don't call me Rosa again, that is no longer my name!*' interrupted the new girl. '*I shall now be known as Camellia!*' She turned to face the growing audience.

'*Last night something incredible happened,*' she proclaimed.

'*That bumbling, bush-headed, fox-lover Rosa walked into some... machine... and worked her nerdy magic. Then out of the other side came – voilà – me. The most perfect girl you will ever see!*'

Rosa shivered. What had she done?

She had created a monster.

From the corner of her eye, Camellia saw Rosa watching her. *'Look who it is, crawling around like an insect: Ro-sa Frank-lin.'*

The other children laughed. *'Ro-sa Frank-lin, Ro-sa Frank-lin, Ro-sa Frank-lin,'* they chanted.

All Rosa could do was watch Camellia glide away, followed by all the other children. She felt like a caterpillar who was never going to become a butterfly.

What was she going to do? The scientists' machine must have corrupted some of her genetic code when it made the Camellia copy. Rosa thought for a while then did what she always did when she had a problem. She headed for the library.

When she came out of the library, at the end of that dreadful day, Rosa was relieved to see that her faithful fox, Dr Watson, was waiting for her. They went straight to the laboratory and peered through the window. The two scientists were there again, only this time they were arguing.

The man was frantically waving his arms around like an out-of-control helicopter, shouting at the woman with the grey-white broomstick hair. *'We don't have permission to do this, Sylvia. Just think of the consequences!'* he cried.

The woman nodded.

'Okay, okay. You're right. We'll have to destroy it.'

This surely wasn't good news for Rosa. *'Dr Watson, wait here. Stall them if you have to. I'll be back as soon as I can,'* she whispered.

As Rosa ran down the street, she could hear yet more chanting. She turned into an alleyway and crashed into a wall of children. They were lined up in front of the very person she was looking for – Camellia.

'*Don't you ever come back here Pandora Peterson!*' she roared.

Pandora appeared from the pack and ran towards Rosa. She looked dreadful. '*Now I know how I made you feel, Rosa. I'm so sorry,*' she sniffled, running away.

'*And you, Rosa, you disastrously dull dingbat,*' Camellia went on, '*how dare you breathe the same air as me!*'

Rosa shook her head in dismay. The scientist's words rang in her ears. '*Now we can create perfect people!*'

It seemed that they still had a long way to go with their machine. Perfect? Camellia wasn't even close!

Rosa thought back to what she'd read in the library earlier. And then it came to her in a flash. She knew how she could get rid of the monster she had created. However, it was going to require some cunning.

'*You might be perfect Camellia, but you're really not that powerful,*' said Rosa. '*Thank goodness those scientists are destroying that machine. Otherwise you could use it to make hundreds of weaker Camellia clones who would always obey you.*'

Camellia's eyes widened. Never one to think twice, she raced to the laboratory and climbed through the open window, closely followed by Rosa. They could hear the chatter of the two scientists in the next room.

Camellia had seconds to act. She leapt into the machine and hit the big red button with an enormous

thwack!

As she listened to the familiar rumble of the machine, Rosa thought back to how she'd felt when she'd been inside it. She had wanted to create a new Rosa – someone who would be like everyone else – a person who didn't live for science books and computer coding. What a crazy idea that had been! These were the things that made her Rosa.

Rosa opened the machine. Camellia had gone. Standing there in her place was a beautiful plant with a vibrant pink and purple flower and the most perfect arrangement of petals Rosa had ever seen.

Camellia had not been copied. She had been transformed. Blinded by self-importance, she never suspected that she might have been tricked.

The next morning a boy came up to Rosa as she was doing a spot of gardening.

'Excuse me,' he said, 'do you know the way to Helix High School? Today's my first day there. Hey, what's that you're planting? What a stunning flower. That Fibonacci spiral is almost impossibly perfect.'

Rosa smiled. '*I go to Helix High too,*' she replied. '*I can walk with you if you like. And this is a camellia plant. My dad once told me that its flower symbolises perfection.*' Rosa thought for a second then continued. '*There was a girl who wanted to be perfect. She was kind of me. Well, I was the caterpillar and she was the butterfly. But now she's this plant.*'

'*Sorry, I didn't understand one bit of that,*' the boy chuckled.

For the first time in what felt like years Rosa laughed too. She felt like she'd been inside a giant cocoon the whole time. But something in her had changed over the last few days. A new and confident Rosa was beginning to emerge.

'*Oh, it's a long story,*' she said. '*I can tell it to you on the way to school. My name's Rosa, by the way.*'

'*I'm Marcus,*' said the boy. '*Very pleased to meet you.*'

As it turned out Rosa and Marcus had lots in common. From then on, they walked to school together every day, chatting excitedly about their latest scientific discoveries.

And Dr Watson?

Well, that's the thing with imaginary
friends, they always know exactly
the right time to move on.